Titles in the **Explore Engineering** Set

 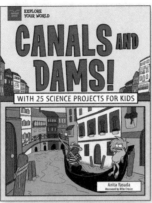  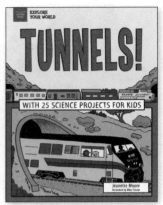

Check out more titles at www.nomadpress.net

Nomad Press
A division of Nomad Communications
10 9 8 7 6 5 4 3 2 1

This book was manufactured by Versa Press,
East Peoria, Illinois
August 2018, Job #J17-12593

ISBN Softcover: 978-1-61930-591-5
ISBN Hardcover: 978-1-61930-587-8

Educational Consultant, Marla Conn

Questions regarding the ordering of this book should be addressed to
Nomad Press
2456 Christian St.
White River Junction, VT 05001
www.nomadpress.net

Printed in the United States of America.

CONTENTS

Interested in primary sources? Look for this icon. Use a smartphone or tablet app to scan the QR code and explore more! Photos are also primary sources because a photograph takes a picture at the moment something happens.

If the QR code doesn't work, there's a list of URLs on the Resources page. Or, try searching the internet with the Keyword Prompts to find other helpful sources.

KEYWORD PROMPTS

bridges 🔍

PREHISTORIC TIMES: Simple bridges consist of a log over a stream.

1600 BCE: A bridge is built over the River Havos in Mycenae, Greece.

850 BCE: A stone arch bridge is built in Izmir, Turkey.

FIRST CENTURY CE: Romans begin building arch bridges.

134 CE: Hadrian's Bridge is built in Rome, Italy. Part of this very strong stone arch bridge is still standing today.

SIXTH CENTURY CE: Zhaozhou Bridge is built in China.

1345: Ponte Vecchio Bridge in Florence, Italy, is built. The inhabited stone arch bridge still has stores on it.

1176–1209: London Bridge is built in England. This is the first arch bridge to be built in tidal waters, which means it has to deal with the rising and lowering of the river tides.

1591: Rialto Bridge in Venice, Italy, is constructed. This stone, inhabited arch bridge is still standing today.

1706: Luding Bridge, the oldest suspension bridge in China, is constructed.

1779: The first iron bridge is built in England. It spans 100 feet.

1866:
The first cantilever bridge is built by Heinrich Gerber in Germany.

1883:
The Brooklyn Bridge is built in New York. It is a cable-stayed suspension bridge.

OCTOBER 2017:
The old Kosciuszko Bridge in New York City is destroyed, replaced by a new bridge, signaling awareness on the part of engineers that old bridges need to be repaired or replaced to keep travel safe for everyone.

1886:
Construction begins on the Tower Bridge in London. It is both a moveable bridge and a suspension bridge.

1923:
Construction begins on the Sydney Harbour Bridge in Australia. It is an arch bridge made completely out of steel.

2008:
The Akashi Kaikyo Bridge in Japan is completed. It is the fourth-tallest bridge and the longest suspension bridge in the world.

1933:
The Golden Gate Bridge is built across the entrance to San Francisco Bay in California. It is a suspension bridge.

2004:
The tallest bridge in the world, the Millau Viaduct in Millau, France, opens. The cable-stayed bridge rises 1,125 feet off the ground.

INTRODUCTION

LET'S EXPLORE BRIDGES

Imagine that you're sitting on the school bus, on your way to school. As the bus bounces along the road, you look up. Huge steel bars and cables rise up around you toward the sky. You tip your head back to see how high they go. What are you looking at? Parts of a bridge! Look down and you'll notice that the bus is crossing something, such as a river.

Bridges connect things. They allow people to move from one place to another more easily. A bridge can cross a road, a narrow valley, or even a body of water.

WORDS TO KNOW

steel: a hard, strong material made of iron combined with other elements.

bridge: a structure built to cross something that blocks your way, such as a river, bay, road, railway, or valley.

1

Bridges pass over lakes and rivers, connect mountains, and cross canyons. There is even a bridge across the Grand Canyon!

Bridges have been around for thousands of years. The ancient Romans first built bridges in the second century BCE. They were built to allow people to cross rivers to trade goods and tell each other news. Roman armies needed these bridges to move from one place to another.

The Romans mostly built bridges using arches to support them. At first, Roman engineers used stone blocks that were held together with iron clamps. These bridges were large and heavy, though, and couldn't span long distances.

The Romans tried using other materials. They mixed broken bits of stone with clay, sand, and water to create something that hardened when it dried, even under water.

What had they invented? The first concrete, which they used to build bridges. Concrete bridges faced with stone were much stronger and easier to build. These bridges also lasted a lot longer. Hundreds of Roman bridges built during and after the second century BCE are still standing.

BRIDGE STRUCTURES TODAY

There are six basic bridge structures in use today. These include beam, truss, arch, cantilever, suspension, and cable. Each type of bridge has a different purpose. Some are stronger than others, some can fit into smaller areas of land, and some just look nicer. Each bridge design is carefully selected for the area where it will stand, what it will carry, and how far it must span.

Have you ever seen a picture of a famous bridge, such as the Golden Gate Bridge in San Francisco or maybe the Sydney Harbour Bridge in Australia? How were these bridges constructed?

THE SYDNEY HARBOUR BRIDGE

GOOD ENGINEERING PRACTICES

Engineers and scientists keep their ideas organized in notebooks. Engineers use the engineering design process to keep track of their inventions, and scientists use the scientific method to keep track of experiments.

As you read through this book and do the activities, record your observations, data, and designs in an engineering design worksheet or a scientific method worksheet. When doing an activity, remember that there is no right answer or right way to approach a project. Be creative and have fun!

Engineering Design Worksheet	Scientific Method Worksheet
Problem: What problem are we trying to solve?	**Question:** What problem are we trying to solve?
Research: Has anything been invented to help solve the problem? What can we learn?	**Research:** What information is already known?
Question: Are there any special requirements for the device? What is it supposed to do?	**Hypothesis/Prediction:** What do I think the answer will be?
Brainstorm: Draw lots of designs for your device and list the materials you are using!	**Equipment:** What supplies do I need?
Prototype: Build the design you drew during brainstorming. This is your prototype.	**Method:** What steps will I follow?
Results: Test your prototype and record your observations.	**Results:** What happened and why?
Evaluate: Analyze your test results. Do you need to make adjustments? Do you need to try a different prototype?	

DID YOU KNOW?

The Nanpu Bridge in Shanghai, China, is in the shape of a spiral. This bridge goes around and around in a circle. It was made that way to save space.

WORDS ᴛᴏ KNOW

feat: an achievement that requires great courage, skill, or strength.

engineering: the use of science and math in the design and construction of things.

stable: steady and firm, not changing.

force: a push or pull applied to an object.

gravity: the force that pulls all objects to the earth's surface.

You might have even tried to build your own bridges with blocks or small wooden sticks. It's not as easy as you might think, is it?

Bridges are feats of engineering that can take years to construct. Building a bridge involves lots of planning and special materials. A bridge has to be strong enough to support the weight of the cars and trucks that cross it every day. It also must be stable enough to withstand extreme weather, such as high winds, floodwater, and earthquakes.

Would you like to learn how to build a bridge? In this book, you will explore how bridges are designed. You'll learn what materials are needed for a strong, stable bridge. Most importantly, you will learn how forces act on bridges to keep them standing or make them fall down.

Become a junior engineer! Performing hands-on experiments will demonstrate the ups and downs, pushes and pulls, and even the gravity-defying properties of bridges. Let's go explore bridges!

WHAT KIND OF CAR CAN DRIVE OVER WATER?

HA HA HA

Any kind, as long as there's a bridge!

SIMPLE BRIDGES FROM ANCIENT TIMES

SUPPLIES

* 2 large blocks or bricks
* ruler
* pieces of construction paper
* several coins
* engineering notebook and pencil

Bridges are not easy to construct. With all of the different types of bridges, it is important to pick the correct one for the area. Let's start with some paper models to get an idea of which shapes are the strongest. Use a scientific method worksheet to stay organized! Start with your question: Which type of paper bridge is strongest?

1 Place one block or brick on each side. Each side should be the same height.

2 Measure the distance between the blocks. Make sure that this distance stays the same for each type of bridge.

3 Place a piece of construction paper across the two bricks to make a simple bridge.

4 How many coins do you think this bridge can support? Your answer is your hypothesis. Stack coins on the paper until it collapses. How many coins could the bridge hold? Record the answer in your engineering notebook.

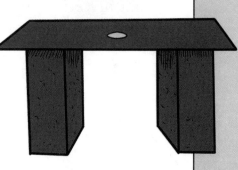

WORDS TO KNOW

collapse: to fall in or down suddenly.

PROJECT!

5 Take another piece of construction paper and fold it up on the sides to make walls on the bridge. Repeat step 4. Was your hypothesis correct?

WALLED BRIDGE

6 Create an arch with a second piece of paper rounded under a horizontal piece. Repeat step 4. Record your data in your notebook.

ARCHED BRIDGE

7 Fold a separate piece of paper like an accordion. Place it on top of the horizontal paper. Place another flat paper on top. Repeat step 4. How strong is this shape of paper?

TRUSS BRIDGE

THINK ABOUT IT: What are your results? Which bridge model can hold the most weight? What is it about this structure that makes it stronger than the others?

ESSENTIAL QUESTIONS

Each chapter of this book begins with an essential question to help guide your exploration of bridges. Keep the question in your mind as you read the chapter. At the end of each chapter, use your engineering notebook to record your thoughts and answers.

?

INVESTIGATE!

Why do we need different types of bridges for different purposes?

CHAPTER 1

WHY DO WE NEED BRIDGES?

Every day, all around the world, buses, cars, and trains use bridges to transport people and goods wherever they need to go. Most of us don't even think about how many bridges we travel over on a daily basis. It's become natural to us. But why do we need bridges?

A bridge is a structure that connects two places. It allows us to reach a road or piece of land. For example, if you need to get across a river or stream, how would you do it without a bridge? You might have to wade through the water or swim, and get very wet in the process! If you build a bridge over the water, you can walk across and stay dry.

? INVESTIGATE!

Why are bridges important? What might the world be like without bridges?

Bridges aren't built over just water—they can also be constructed over valleys, rough and rocky land, or even over other roads.

EARLY BRIDGES

Bridges aren't always long and complex. A small wooden plank or tree branch stretched across a river can make a bridge to the other side. Some bridges are even made by nature itself. These are called natural bridges.

Natural bridges are created when a tree falls across a river or other obstacle by itself. Natural bridges can also be made out of rock when water erodes, or breaks down, the center of the rock, forming bridges that people can

cross. Humans have been using natural bridges since they first started moving from one place to another. Have you ever crossed a natural bridge?

natural bridge: a bridge created by the natural formation of rock or land.

pedestrian: a person walking to get from one place to another.

obstacle: something that blocks you from what you want to achieve.

erode: to wear away rock or soil by water and wind.

WORDS TO KNOW

DID YOU KNOW?

There are bridges that are just for people! These are usually called pedestrian or foot bridges.

9

Eventually, humans realized that natural bridges weren't enough. A natural bridge allows people to cross only where the bridge forms. People began building their own bridges at the places they wanted to cross.

The first bridges date back more than 4,000 years. These were constructed with small bits of timber, logs, and rough planks. The wood was held together with dirt that was packed tightly around it. Wood was the best material available to early civilizations to build bridges.

These wooden and dirt bridges were not very strong. They couldn't hold much weight and could span only very short distances. During heavy rains, the bridges usually collapsed because the rain washed away the dirt.

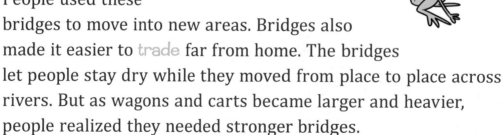

DID YOU KNOW?

The earliest known stone bridge in Europe was built around 1900 BCE at the Palace of Knossos, Crete.

Still, the early bridges served their purpose. People used these bridges to move into new areas. Bridges also made it easier to trade far from home. The bridges let people stay dry while they moved from place to place across rivers. But as wagons and carts became larger and heavier, people realized they needed stronger bridges.

MAKING STRONGER BRIDGES

As time went by, civilizations developed new materials to make bridges stronger and more durable. This was necessary because people began to use carts with stone wheels when they traveled. Wooden bridges couldn't hold the weight of these heavy carts going over them day after day.

durable: lasting a long time.

mortar: a building material that hardens when it dries, like glue. It is used to hold bricks and stones together.

volcanic: from lava that came out of a volcano.

WORDS TO KNOW

Wooden bridges were also not sturdy enough to span long distances. As cities grew, the people who lived there did more trading and the goods had to be moved greater distances. Longer, stronger bridges were necessary to keep up with the growth of cities and communities.

Ancient Roman engineers set to work trying to solve the problem. They knew stone bridges were much stronger than wooden ones, but how could they make the rocks stick together? Dirt was easily washed away by rain.

Their solution was mortar, a paste made of crushed volcanic rocks. With mortar, the Romans were able to build longer, more durable bridges that spanned entire rivers and streams. Transportation increased and territories expanded. Soon, people were exchanging information with others in lands they had never been able to reach before.

For many centuries in Europe, stone bridges were used everywhere. In fact, some stone bridges became a type of house. During the twelfth to sixteenth centuries CE, inhabited bridges were very popular.

An inhabited bridge is a bridge that has tiny houses built along its edges. One of the most famous inhabited bridges is London Bridge in England. This bridge is still standing, although no people live on it.

DID YOU KNOW?

The world's longest bridge over water is the Lake Pontchartrain Causeway in Louisiana. The causeway is constructed of two bridges right next to each other. The longest one is about 24 miles long.

Some civilizations had to rely on different materials for their bridges. The Incas in Peru were known to make amazing bridges that stretched across mountains and spanned valleys as wide as 150 feet. These bridges were made with rope.

Rope bridges can be quite strong, but they wobble back and forth when you walk across them. The handrails are just long pieces of rope and aren't very steady! The bridges did their job, however—they allowed communities to move around and trade goods and information.

While stone bridges from the past still exist, in 1779, the new material for bridges was iron. This very strong material is capable of withstanding extreme weather for many years. Technology had developed enough so that iron could be cast into curved shapes for arched bridges. The pieces were attached with sturdy rivets and fit together, kind of like puzzle pieces. While iron is very strong and seems inflexible, these new bridges appeared to be light and modern.

LET'S REBUILD A BRIDGE

None of the rope bridges built by the Incas have survived to present day. But each year, in a town called Huinchiri, Peru, people gather to re-build the Keshwa Chaca Bridge. They take grasses that grow along the road and weave them into 164-foot lengths. They attach smaller ropes as the cables and stretch the whole thing across the Apurmac River. The new bridge lasts until the re-building in the following year. What a great way to learn about engineering while keeping a culture alive!

You can watch people rebuilding the bridge in this video. Why is this bridge important to them?

KEYWORD PROMPTS

Keshwa Chaca Bridge video

WORDS TO KNOW

maintenance: to keep something working and in good shape.

infrastructure: roads, bridges, and other basic types of structures and equipment needed for a country to function properly.

interconnected: when two or more things are related or have an impact on each other.

Beginning in the late 1800s, iron gave way to steel, an even stronger and more durable material. Today, many bridges are constructed with steel. It can be shaped into any style and size and lasts for many years with maintenance. Concrete is also used to support and cover some of the steel sections on some bridges.

Bridges allow easy travel across every type of landform, from rivers and lakes to valleys and rocky landscapes. Today, bridges carry millions of cars, trucks, buses, and trains from city to city, across state lines, and beyond countries—even joining continents.

Bridges are important for trade, travel, shipping, communication, and culture. They are a huge part of the infrastructure, or system of transportation, of every major country. The world would not be as interconnected as it is without bridges.

? CONSIDER AND DISCUSS

It's time to consider and discuss: Why are bridges important? What might the world be like without bridges?

COOPERATION BUILDS A BRIDGE

When people work together, they can often make things that are larger and better than if one person works alone! See what you and your friends can come up with to cross a stretch of flowing lava together. Use the engineering design process. What problem are you trying to solve? How to get many people across a river of lava!

SUPPLIES

* engineering notebook and pencil
* large empty room
* tape measure
* masking tape
* 6–8 people
* 12 sheets of newspaper, folded in half

1 Mark off 8 to 10 feet on the floor of the room. Put a piece of masking tape at both ends. This is the journey you must take. Pretend the floor is made of hot, flowing lava that you can't touch!

2 Split the people into two equal groups to form teams. Brainstorm ideas for getting across the lava using the newspapers. Think up lots of options.

3 Each team takes turns trying their ideas. When something doesn't work, figure out why and try a different way!

THINK ABOUT IT: How would you have gotten across by yourself? Can you design a method that works for one person? Is it harder or easier?

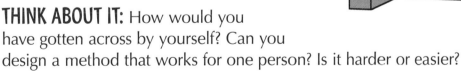

THROW ME A ROPE!

Have you ever seen a movie where the main character has to cross a tiny bridge made of rope? It sways from side to side as they walk, and even bounces the person up and down. Makes you think twice about wanting to cross, doesn't it? Build your own rope bridge and test its strength.

SUPPLIES

* 4 large bricks with holes
* ruler
* kite string or other type of strong string (not fishing line)
* scissors
* objects with weight

1 Lay one brick on its side. Set another brick on top of it. Both bricks should have their openings facing the same way. Repeat with the second set of bricks. Place the brick sets about 8 to 10 inches apart.

2 Cut the string into 26 pieces that are each at least 18 inches long. Weave two pieces of string into one by twisting them around and around each other.

3 Take this 18-inch double string and tie one end around the middle of the holes in the bottom brick. Tie the other end in the same place in the other brick set. Make sure the string is tight. This is the bottom of your rope bridge.

4 Weave two more pieces of string into one by twisting them around and around each other.

5 Tie one end of the double string around the outside of the left side of the top brick. Fasten in the same spot on the other brick.

6 Repeat step 5 and put the double string around the outside of the right side of the top brick. These three strings make the basis of your rope bridge.

7 Take a string and fasten the end to one of the double strings. Tie it in the middle to the bottom string. Tie the other ends to the other double strings. This is how your rope bridge gets its support.

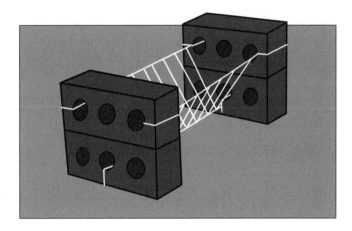

8 Repeat with all of your remaining strings. You should end up with something like the bridge in this picture.

9 Test the bridge by placing weighted objects on it, such as building blocks, marshmallows, and plastic cups. How does the bridge behave? Does it move? Why?

THINK ABOUT IT: While it might be scary to cross a rope bridge that moves, rope bridges have many benefits. They are easy to take down, they use readily available materials, and sometimes, they can be removed and then put back up if needed. Can you think of other good things about rope bridges?

MATERIAL MATCH-UP

The material that is used to make a bridge plays a big part in its strength and durability. In a previous experiment, we used paper. Now let's see how a thicker material such as cardboard works.

1 Lay a piece of cardboard on the floor. Place two books on each side, slightly closer together than the length of cardboard.

2 Place one piece of cardboard between the two books to form a bridge.

3 Add another book to both stacks so the piece of cardboard is supported above and below with books.

4 Repeat steps 1–3 using the construction paper instead of the cardboard. You are going to conduct two experiments at the same time to test materials.

DID YOU KNOW?

One aspect of planning a bridge in ancient Rome was easy. Roman law said every road must be "8 feet wide where straight and 16 feet when curved." A bridge needed to be wide enough to fit the road on it.

PROJECT!

5 Using the ruler, find the midpoint between the books. The midpoint of any bridge can be the weakest point because it is farthest from the supports

6 Place your weighted objects (coins, beans, or race cars) in the midpoint of both bridges.

7 Keep adding weight until the bridge breaks. Which bridge material was stronger? Record your observations in your journal.

TRY THIS: Repeat this experiment with the arch design and the truss design from the project on pages 6 and 7. Which material is strongest in each type of bridge?

LONDON BRIDGE IS FALLING DOWN

You might be familiar with the nursery rhyme "London Bridge is Falling Down." But did you know that song refers to an actual bridge in London? In fact, there have been three bridges called London Bridge. The first was an arch bridge built in 1176. By the 1300s, it was an inhabited bridge and home to more than 144 shops. The bridge was damaged in the Great Fire in 1666 and closed. In 1820, a new London Bridge was built. This one was used until 1960, when a third London Bridge was built. The second bridge was taken down, stone by stone and sent to Arizona. London Bridge is now in the United States!

CHAPTER 2

ENGINEERING AND DESIGN

• • • • • • • • • •   • • • • • • • • •

Designing and building a bridge is a hard job. It's part science and part art. The bridge must be strong enough to handle thousands of cars and trucks during its lifetime. It must be able to stand up to high heat and icy cold. It also needs to survive high winds, flooding, and natural disasters such as earthquakes and tornadoes!

• •

How does wind, rain, and extreme temperature affect a bridge? All of these things apply forces to the bridge. A force is a push or pull on an object. Forces act on everything—cars, trucks, planes, bridges, even you!

? INVESTIGATE!

What do engineers need to think about when they design a bridge?

Gravity is an example of a force. What happens when you toss a ball in the air? Gravity is the force that brings that ball back down to the ground! Gravity pulls everything toward the center of the planet. This is also one of the major forces that act upon a bridge.

All structures, including houses, skyscrapers, and bridges, have forces acting on them. Forces can push, pull, twist, or bend. When an engineer designs a bridge, they need to understand how all of the different forces will act upon it. In order to do that, they must answer the following questions.

* Where will the bridge be built?

* How will it be used?

* How much and what kind of traffic will it need to handle?

* What type of weather is in the area?

NATURE IS A BRIDGE'S GREATEST ENEMY

You might think that a little rain isn't a big deal to a huge steel bridge. Well, it's not. But when that little bit of rain becomes a torrential downpour and water rises to flood stage, it becomes much more dangerous. Floods are one of the most common causes of bridge collapse. The huge force of rushing water can eat away a bridge's footings. Once the bridge becomes unstable, the rest of it is easily torn apart.

compression: a pushing force that squeezes or presses a material inward.

tension: a pulling force that pulls or stretches a material outward.

load: an object that puts weight on another object.

torsion: a twisting force that turns or twirls a material.

shear: a sliding force that slips parts of a material in opposite directions.

foundation: the supporting part of a structure, found usually at the bottom.

WORDS TO KNOW

The answers to these questions will tell the engineer what type of forces will be acting on their bridge. There are five forces that bridge engineers need to be concerned with: compression, tension, load, torsion, and shear.

Let's take a look at each of these forces.

COMPRESSION

Compression is the force an object feels when it is being squeezed. Gravity pulls down on the bridge while the foundations of the bridge push back up. This squeeze is the compression force, and the bridge material, whether it is wood or steel, feels it.

For a bridge to remain standing, the compression force needs to be balanced. The force pulling down needs to equal the force pushing up. If one or the other becomes too great, the bridge can collapse.

DID YOU KNOW?

Steel is a great material for bridges because it has the same compression and tension strength, which balance each other. Steel can also be bent into any shape.

Compression forces can also cause the materials in the bridge to buckle. Compression is an inward force that can form wrinkles, called buckling. As the bridge material buckles, the bridge becomes weaker and can collapse.

buckle: to collapse in the middle.

WORDS TO KNOW

TENSION

Tension is the opposite of compression. While compression is a force that pushes inward, tension is a force that pulls out. If the tension force within the steel or wood becomes too great, the material will snap, causing the bridge to collapse.

Tension and compression are the two main forces that keep bridges standing. These are also the forces that can make a bridge fall down, which is why it is extremely important for engineers to understand how they work!

WHAT KIND OF JAM ISN'T GOOD TO EAT?

HA HA HA

A traffic jam!

BUCKLING BUILDINGS

Just like bridges, buildings can also collapse because of buckling. That can happen when the middle supports of the building are suddenly weakened by fire or impact. If the load becomes too great for these supports to hold, they can buckle.

23

DID YOU KNOW?

The Brooklyn Bridge of New York joins Manhattan and Brooklyn over the East River. When completed in 1883, it was the longest suspension bridge in the world. It features average daily traffic of about 145,000 vehicles.

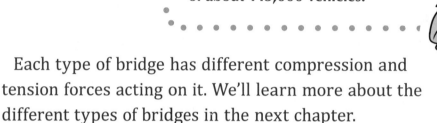

Each type of bridge has different compression and tension forces acting on it. We'll learn more about the different types of bridges in the next chapter.

LOAD

When a bridge is empty, all it needs to do is support its own weight. That is not as easy as it sounds! The crossbeams, the road, and the materials are all quite heavy. These make up what is called the dead load of the bridge. The dead load is the total weight of the bridge itself.

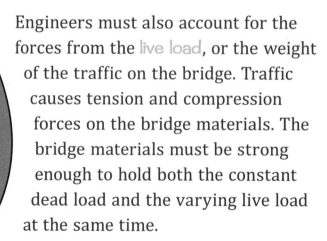

Engineers must also account for the forces from the live load, or the weight of the traffic on the bridge. Traffic causes tension and compression forces on the bridge materials. The bridge materials must be strong enough to hold both the constant dead load and the varying live load at the same time.

beam: a rigid piece of the structure that carries the load.

WORDS ⏆ KNOW

TORSION

Torsion is a twisting force. On a bridge, torsion can be caused by high winds or the movement of the beams that support the bridge. During hurricanes, tornadoes, or even just bad storms, high winds have been known to twist bridges at either end. The twisting forces can become great enough to collapse the bridge.

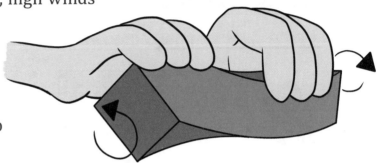

One of the most famous bridge collapses was the Tacoma Narrows Bridge in Washington state. The bridge experienced movement from the very first day it opened! Travelers crossing the bridge complained they felt seasick after driving over it, even on a day without wind.

On November 7, 1940, wind gusts of 40 miles per hour hit the bridge. It began to sway so badly that the bridge supports buckled and collapsed. The torsion force was too much.

(PS) **Watch the Tacoma Narrows Bridge collapse at this website.** What forces can you see working on the bridge in this video? What might engineers have done while designing the bridge to prevent this kind of collapse?

KEYWORD PROMPTS

Tacoma Narrows Bridge collapse 🔍

SHEAR

Shear is a sliding force. This force occurs when the bridge materials are being pulled in two different directions. Shear occurs between two beams on a bridge that are connected at an angle. It causes the material to snap, crack, and break apart.

Bridges experience shear during high winds and floods or when any part of the material becomes weak. A weakened beam will not carry its load properly and can cause the bridge to fail.

Understanding how forces work is very important when building a bridge. Engineers go to school and take many classes to learn about them. It is a huge responsibility to build a bridge.

DID YOU KNOW?

When engineers are designing bridges, they will sometimes build a complete bridge on a smaller scale to test it in a wind tunnel. They want to be sure that the bridge will stand up to forces from high winds.

FORCES THAT CAN TOPPLE A BRIDGE

Engineers have to understand the types of forces that nature can apply to a bridge. Some of them, such as rising water, are quite dangerous. Water that has risen even a few feet can have a huge impact on a bridge. Floods are one of the most frequent causes of bridge collapse. Most bridges are built over some type of water—a stream, lake, river, or estuary. The real problem comes when the water gets so high that it sweeps by as a massive flood! Fast-moving water has a great deal of force. That force can be strong enough to knock a part of the pier off its support.

In a flood, it's not just the water that is the danger. When floods happen, they usually carry a lot of debris. Downed trees, bits of buildings, even boats and cars can all be pushed into a bridge. The impact from the debris can cause a lot of damage to the bridge structure.

WORDS TO KNOW

estuary: a partly enclosed coastal body of water, which has rivers and streams flowing into it and is connected to the ocean.

pier: a supporting pillar or post.

debris: the remains of anything broken down or destroyed.

soil composition: the bits of minerals, rocks, and dirt that are present in the soil.

BECOME AN ENGINEER!

People who build bridges are called civil engineers. Civil engineers help the public by creating buildings, roads, and bridges. Engineers study for at least four years at a college or university and take classes in physics, mathematics, and engineering principles. They also learn about materials and soil composition.

BRIDGES!

SAFETY FIRST!

The majority of all bridges are safe because they are inspected on a regular basis. An inspection team goes to each bridge and assigns it a rating. If the rating is good, or high, the bridge is not re-inspected for two to three years. If the rating is low, then the bridge might be re-inspected the following year. Bridges that don't pass the rating system are marked for immediate repair.

When inspectors look at a bridge, they evaluate its safety and security. They ask lots of questions.

DID YOU KNOW?

Most bridges are inspected every two years. During inspection, a bridge is checked for wear and damage.

✳ Is the original design still intact?

✳ Does the bridge appear to have all its original parts in place?

✳ Is it able to handle the amount of traffic that goes over it?

✳ Is the bridge superstructure, the part supporting the bridge deck, still secured?

✳ Is the substructure, the parts supporting the underside of the bridge, good as well?

WHO INSPECTS THE BRIDGES?

The U.S. Department of Transportation (DOT) is run by the federal government. This organization oversees the federal roads and bridges and receives reports from every state. Each state has its own DOT. There are also individual bridge authorities and transportation commissions within a state. The main goal of all of these agencies is to ensure the safety of the bridges and roads. It's a big job! For example, in New York, there are 65 different teams that inspect about 9,500 bridges and highways every year.

All of these answers are evaluated and a rating is given. The rating can be based on 100 percent, where 100 is a perfect bridge and zero is an extremely dangerous bridge. Bridges are thought to be good if they are at 70 percent or above. Anything below 40 percent is in poor condition.

While some bridges suffer terrible accidents, many bridges last for a long, long time! In the next chapter, we'll take a look at the different types of bridges engineers are building today—beam, truss, arch, cantilever, suspension, and cable.

We'll find out why engineers choose certain types of bridges for different locations.

? CONSIDER AND DISCUSS

It's time to consider and discuss: What do engineers need to think about when they design a bridge?

FEEL THE FORCE

Every bridge must be solid enough to withstand the forces that act on it. But how strong are those forces? This short exercise will give you an idea.

1 Face your partner with a little less than an arm's length between you. Grab hands with your partner.

2 Each of you should lean slightly backward. Do you feel the pull on your arms? That is tension. Tension is a force that happens to all bridges.

3 Stand upright. Now, place your palms against your partner's palms.

4 Lean in toward your partner. What do you feel? This is compression, another force that is present in all bridges.

TRY THIS: Ask an adult to try this with you. Can you hold them up as easily as you held up your friend? How does this relate to the bridge?

DID YOU KNOW?

Sometimes the material used for a bridge has flaws. In 1967, a bridge collapsed in Ohio due to a manufacturing defect in a piece of chain. The bridge was weak in one area and couldn't handle the load. Crash!

PROJECT!

PROJECT TWIST AND TURN

SUPPLIES

* 3 pieces of balsa wood
* scissors
* ruler

In addition to compression and tension, torsion and shear forces also need to be considered when building a bridge. These forces are caused by high winds or extreme weather.

1 Take your pieces of balsa wood and cut them into three pieces this long: 6 inches, 12 inches, and 18 inches.

2 Hold the 6-inch piece between the forefingers of each hand. Twist your fingers on each hand in a different direction. What happens to the wood? This motion is caused by torsion.

3 Repeat with the 12-inch and 18-inch pieces of wood. What happens? Does the torsion force increase or decrease with length?

4 Now, hold the 6-inch piece of wood in both of your fists. Pull back with one hand while you push forward with the other. What happens? Does it break?

5 Repeat with the other pieces. What happens? This force is shear. Shear is not dependent upon length, but upon strength of the material.

THINK ABOUT IT: What other materials could you try that would not break if you applied the shear force? Hint: Try paper towel rolls and straws! What else can you find?

PUSH AND PULL

SUPPLIES

✳ 3 pieces of balsa wood
✳ scissors
✳ ruler

The two most important forces on a bridge are compression and tension. This experiment will show you how each force acts on a single beam of a bridge.

1 Cut the balsa wood into different sizes: 6 inches, 12 inches, 18 inches.

2 Place the 6-inch piece of wood with the two ends in the middle of each palm.

3 Push in with your palms. What happens? Does the wood bend or break?

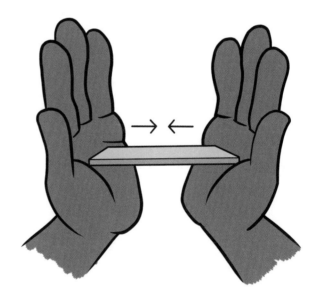

4 Repeat with the 12-inch and 18-inch pieces. As the pieces of wood get longer, what do you notice? Does the wood begin to bend?

5 Now, hold the 6-inch piece of wood between the forefingers of each hand.

6 Pull outward on the wood. What happens? Does it move?

7 Repeat with the 12-inch and 18-inch pieces of wood. What happens? Does the wood stretch or does it stay the same?

THINK MORE: Consider the balsa wood as a piece of a bridge. How do you think the bridge would act if it were able to be stretched or compressed like the piece of balsa? Would it move? Or break?

EARTHQUAKE!

Earthquakes can cause major damage to bridges. An earthquake happens when the ground shifts unexpectedly because two pieces of the earth's crust, known as tectonic plates, move against each other. Any structure on that land will naturally feel the vibrations of the move. If the materials of the bridge are able to stretch and bend like the balsa wood, they may not break. However, balsa wood isn't strong enough to hold up a car, never mind a tractor-trailer truck! That's why engineers are working hard to develop new materials that can be used to build bridges that bounce back into shape after an earthquake. One new bridge that's being planned for Seattle, Washington, will have steel columns around rods of material made from nickel and titanium. These rods will be able to flex and bend and then return to their original shape. This new kind of bridge will also have supports made from a flexible kind of concrete that won't break or crumble when bent or shaken.

LIVE LOAD VS. DEAD LOAD

A bridge must be strong enough to handle its dead load, the weight of the bridge itself, and also the live load, which is the amount of weight that goes over it every day. See how each affects the other.

1 Brainstorm a bridge that uses paper towel rolls and straws. What shape will your bridge take? What forces are affecting your bridge design?

2 Use the paper punch to make holes in the paper towel rolls to slide in the straws. These are your supports.

3 Now attach the piece of balsa wood to straws, just like the deck of a bridge. You can use the tape to secure it, or just rest it on top of them. Does your bridge stand up? Can it support the deck? If so, good. That is your dead load.

4 Now you will test your bridge for live load. Remember, live load is considered to be the weight of the objects that move across the bridge. For this you can use cars or other objects. Start by placing cars (or whatever your load will be) one at a time on top of the deck.

5 Keep adding cars until the bridge begins to sag. Make a note of when the sagging occurs. That is the maximum live load for your bridge. If you want to see it in action, try moving the cars across the bridge. How many cars can the bridge handle? Can it support more cars when they are sitting still or when they are moving?

CHAPTER 3

TYPES OF BRIDGES

When engineers design a bridge, they think about what forces will be acting on it. They consider the location of the bridge and the typical weather, as well as the amount of traffic the bridge needs to support.

Designing a bridge is a complicated task. Luckily, engineers have six basic designs to choose from. Let's take a look at each design.

? INVESTIGATE!

How do engineers decide what type of bridge to build?

beam bridge: a bridge with a horizontal beam across two vertical supports.

horizontal: straight across from side to side.

vertical: straight up and down.

deck: the horizontal part of a bridge, where the cars go over.

interval: a standard space between objects.

WORDS TO KNOW

BEAM BRIDGE

A beam bridge is the most basic form of bridge. It is created by placing a beam horizontally over two vertical posts—easy!

The horizontal part is called the beam, or deck. The vertical posts, or piers, stand upright at either end of the beam. Have you ever made this kind of bridge?

• DID YOU KNOW? •

The longest continuous bridge over water in the world is the 24-mile beam bridge over the Lake Pontchartrain Causeway in Louisiana. To keep it strong, horizontal supports are used at intervals of 56 feet apart throughout the entire length.

Beam bridges are great to cross short distances. The longer the bridge, the weaker it becomes because the vertical supports are far apart. Beam bridges that cross longer distances need supports at regular intervals to keep the bridge strong. Try it yourself with some blocks and pieces of cardboard!

TRUSS BRIDGE

To make beam bridges longer and stronger, engineers add trusses. These are extra support beams that are set at a diagonal to the vertical piers and the horizontal beam. They look like triangles on the sides or top of the bridge.

Trusses help to spread out the weight of the load. Instead of the force being completely supported by just the beam, the truss takes some of the force.

trusses: diagonal beams added to a bridge for extra support.

diagonal: a straight line joining two opposite corners of a square, rectangle, or other straight-sided shape.

truss bridge: a bridge design that uses diagonal posts above or below the bridge to provide extra support.

railway bridge: a bridge that is built to carry trains.

WORDS TO KNOW

Truss bridges are often used when heavy vehicles will be traveling across them. Trusses are almost always added to a railway bridge.

Sometimes, the truss is above the deck, while other times it is below the deck. It might look like a square, a triangle, or even a semicircle.

PROS AND CONS OF A TRUSS BRIDGE

When deciding whether to use a truss bridge, engineers need to take the following factors into consideration.

Advantages:

* They are cheaper

* They are strong and can be built in difficult places

* The deck sits directly on the truss bridge, for added support

Disadvantages:

* They have a complicated design and are heavy

* Building them can create a lot of waste in materials

* Their many parts require a lot of maintenance

CANTILEVER BRIDGE

Adding trusses doesn't always make a bridge strong enough. How could engineers solve this problem? They came up with a cantilever.

Have you ever seen a balcony on the outside of a building? The balcony simply appears to hang in the air, right off the building. Actually, its support is directly underneath it. A cantilever bridge does the same thing.

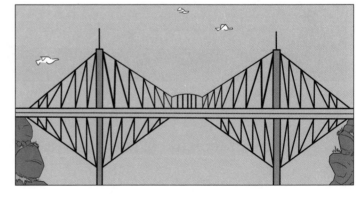

Originally, cantilever bridges were built using wood, but now they are made of reinforced concrete, iron, or steel. Every cantilever bridge has two cantilevers and sometimes a suspended central truss. This truss allows the bridge to be longer and still be safe.

ARCH BRIDGE

The arch bridge has been around for thousands of years. The bridge gets its name from the arch, or curve, that makes a half-circle at the top. The arch connects two piers, or abutments, which support the deck of the bridge.

cantilever bridge: a bridge that uses diagonal cantilever supports, and sometimes trusses.

reinforced concrete: concrete that contains iron bars to make it stronger.

suspended central truss: a truss section added to the middle of a bridge for extra support.

arch bridge: a bridge formed with a curved support as its main component.

abutment: a structure on which a bridge rests, such as a pier.

WORDS ⊙ KNOW

Arch bridges are strong because the curved design spreads the force equally across the entire underside of the deck. That means the bridge is better able to absorb the compression forces of the trains or cars that pass over it. Arch bridges are so strong that they don't need the additional support of a truss or a cantilever.

Natural arches are found all over the world. They are made when wind or water erodes dirt or sand and leaves behind an arch made of rock. **You can see photographs of famous natural arches at this website.**

KEYWORD PROMPTS
Amusing Planet natural arches

The curved design is considered quite beautiful. In fact, arches are often used in buildings, monuments, and even company logos. The next time you watch television or look through a magazine, keep your eyes out for arches!

SUSPENSION BRIDGE

Suspension bridges are great examples of art and engineering working together. Solid rock or concrete anchorages serve as stable foundations for the massive towers that soar high into the sky. The supporting cables swoop up and down from the tops of the towers to the deck below in graceful curves. These cables support the deck and the weight of the load. The Golden Gate Bridge, one of the most famous bridges in the United States, is a suspension bridge.

Building a suspension bridge can be a bit tricky. The anchorages need to be placed deep in the ground. The towers rest on the anchorages, which is why the anchorages must be so large and strong.

Next come the main cables, which must be lifted in place to the top of the towers. The massive cables are held in place by the suspender cables, the vertical lines of cable that stretch between the main cable and the deck.

DID YOU KNOW?

The first suspension bridges were built by the Incas. They used twisted grass to create the supporting cables.

41

The main cables are responsible for keeping the deck stable. The deck is suspended from the main cables. Many suspension bridges have deck trusses added to them. These are diagonal beams of steel set up in triangles and attached to the underside of the deck. This keeps the deck rigid and prevents it from swaying and rippling from weather forces.

CABLE-STAYED BRIDGE

Cable-stayed bridges have been around since the sixteenth century. A cable-stayed bridge can look very similar to a suspension bridge, but it is quite different.

They are faster and easier to construct than suspension bridges. They are best for spanning a distance that's more than 3,000 feet. This is because the way the cables are placed along the sides of the deck make it great for supporting a heavy load.

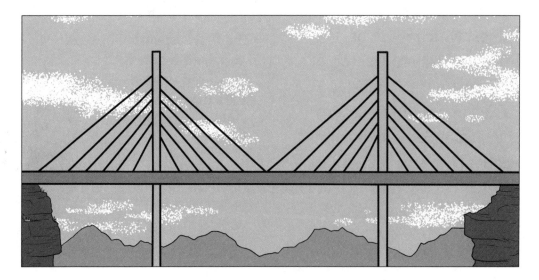

WHAT KIND OF BRIDGE CAN YOU MAKE ON PAPER?

HA HA HA

A Draw Bridge.

Also, cable-stayed bridges use a lot less material than suspension bridges, which makes them much less expensive.

The anchorages on a cable-stayed bridge are thinner and lighter and don't need to be sunk as deeply as those of a suspension bridge. A cable-stayed bridge uses only one set of cables because it balances the load evenly between the towers that support the deck. The cables are pulled tight to provide tension and so they can absorb the compression as the traffic passes over.

Picking a bridge design is not easy! It requires an understanding of the characteristics of each bridge. But making the decision is only part of the process. After the bridge is designed, the real work begins!

In the next chapter, we'll see how civil engineers, workers, and construction companies come together to create amazing bridges that span rivers, lakes, and even small parts of the ocean.

CONSIDER AND DISCUSS

It's time to consider and discuss: How do engineers decide what type of bridge to build?

MAKE A BEAM BRIDGE

Beam bridges are simple to make. All you need are two bases and something to go over the obstacle. Use the engineering design process to build a beam bridge and see if you can improve that bridge to support lots of weight!

SUPPLIES

* ✳ engineering notebook and pencil
* ✳ 2 textbooks
* ✳ balsa wood
* ✳ connecting building blocks
* ✳ construction paper
* ✳ small objects for weight, such as toy cars or rocks

1 Place the textbooks a short distance apart. Lay the balsa wood or construction paper across the two books. You have created a beam bridge. Test your bridge with weights. How much weight can it hold?

2 Try constructing a bridge with the connecting building blocks. Put the blocks together to make a flat deck and place your deck across the textbooks. Test your bridge with weights. Can this hold more or less weight than a bridge made out of paper or balsa wood?

3 Brainstorm ways to make your bridge stronger and more stable. What other materials can you add to reach your goals? Is there a different deck material that would make your bridge really strong?

TRY THIS: Challenge yourself to build a low bridge that can hold your own weight! What will you use for the deck? What will you use for supports? Get creative and try lots of different materials. Test your bridge and try again if it collapses.

ADD THAT SUPPORT!

Vertical supports under a long beam bridge keep the compression forces spread out across the entire beam. Most importantly, it keeps the bridge from sagging in the middle.

PROJECT!

ARCH SUPPORT

SUPPLIES

* engineering notebook and pencil
* ruler
* cardboard
* scissors
* 4 textbooks

You have probably seen the curved supports, called arches, in many different places. Now's the time to use the engineering design process to try to make your own!

1 Cut a strip of cardboard about 14 inches long and 2 inches wide. Bend the strip of cardboard into a long, low arch. Set it on the table. Does it stand upright?

2 Put your finger in the middle of the cardboard and push down. What happens?

DID YOU KNOW?

The second-leading cause of bridge collapse is being hit by a boat or car.

3 Make two stacks of two textbooks each and place them about 10 inches apart.

4 Slide 2 inches of cardboard between the books on each side, creating an arch.

5 Now, push down on the arch with your finger. What happens? What does this tell you about the strength of arch bridges?

THINK MORE: Where is the best place to put a heavy object on an arch bridge? In the middle? On either end? Test your hypothesis!

TRUSSES AT WORK!

Trusses add support to a bridge, and they look cool, too. Give them a try and see how they work.

1 Lay four popsicle sticks flat in a square and glue each corner where two sticks meet.

2 Glue one wooden cube on top of each corner.

3 Repeat steps 1 and 2 to make another square. Each square should have four cubes on it.

4 Take one square and glue three more sticks to it to make a rectangle. It should have two squares attached together to make one rectangle with seven sticks, like the diagram. Glue a stick diagonally through each square.

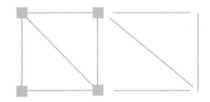

SO MANY TRUSSES

In the 1800s, during the height of railway bridge building, many different engineers invented their own style of truss bridge. They named them after themselves, too. That is why we have the Fink and Bollman, the Lenticular, the Whipple, the Kellogg, the Pegram, and the Schwedler bridges. Only the Pratt, Petit, and Warren truss bridge styles are built today.

5 Glue two cubes on the two new corners of the rectangle. This is your base for the bridge.

6 The other square is for the top of the bridge. Attach it to the base with four new popsicle sticks. Glue them diagonally from the bottom of one square to the square on the top. This will make two triangles on one side. Repeat for the other side of the bridge.

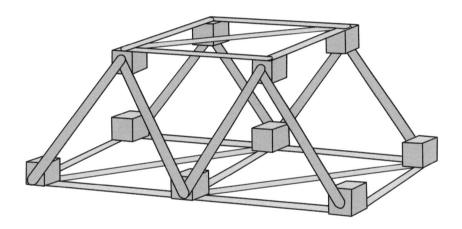

7 Add a flat piece of balsa wood along the top of the base to make the road.

8 Evaluate your bridge by testing the prototype. Add small racecars, trucks, or other objects to see how it holds them up.

9 Does your bridge stay standing? Do you need to develop a new prototype? Brainstorm what you would do. Then try it out!

TRY THIS: Test different forces on the bridge—compression, tension, and torsion. What happens with each force?

SUSPEND IT!

Bridges need support, but did you ever think that support could come from wires (or strings)? Use the engineering design process to give this suspension thing a try!

1 Using the materials you have, brainstorm a way to create a suspension bridge. Draw it out on a piece of paper. Now give it a try.

2 Pull your chairs or stacks of books about 12 inches apart. Take two straws and push them together to make one longer one (about 14 inches in total).

3 Place the straw so that each end is resting on a support. This is your deck straw. Tape down the ends with masking tape.

4 Cut 3 inches off each of two of the other straws. These are your towers. Make a slit at the top of each of your tower straws. This will hold the string that is acting as a cable.

5 Bend the end of each tower down slightly so that you can tape it to the support right next to the end of the deck straw. The towers should be standing upright.

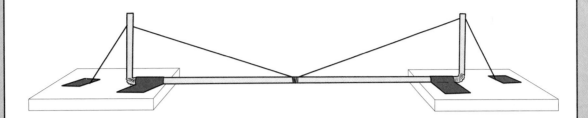

6 Take the long piece of string and attach one end about 4 inches out from the end of the bridge on the support. Tape it down.

7 Loop the rest of it up and through the first tower, down and around the beam straw three or four times, up and through the second tower and pull tight. Tape it down about 4 inches out from the other end of the beam straw.

8 You now have a suspension bridge prototype. To test its strength, hang the paper clip around the middle of the beam straw. Attach a piece of string through the plastic cup and hang it off the paper clip. Add in anything you want as weights, such as pennies, dice, rice, or small stones.

9 Evaluate how your bridge is working. Is it staying up? Do you need to make a new prototype? Brainstorm ideas on how you could improve the bridge.

THINK MORE: How strong is the suspension bridge compared to the other types of bridges you built?

CABLE-STAYED BRIDGE

This bridge is similar to the suspension bridge, except that the cables are in a different pattern. Give this fancy cable-stayed bridge a try! Use the same supplies as you did for the suspension bridge, and follow the first four steps in that project.

1 With the towers built and in place, cut the long piece of string into 8-inch pieces. These will be your cables. Place a knot at the end of each of the 8-inch cables.

2 Set the knot inside the slit at the top of each of the towers. Pull the other end of the string tight and tie it off at an angle to the beam straw. Repeat, going in the opposite direction. Do these same steps for the other tower.

3 Test your bridge to see how much weight it will hold, just as you did with the suspension bridge. Try adding extra strings or shorter and longer pieces to support the beam straw. What happens?

THINK MORE: Does the length of the cables matter? Does the number of cables matter? How can you construct your bridge to hold more weight?

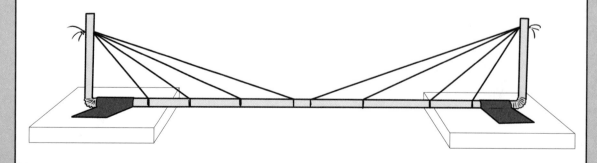

BALANCING ACT

The goal of a cantilever bridge is to balance all of the load of the bridge on one support. Does this sound like an easy task? Use the engineering design process to try it!

1 Stand both shoeboxes upright about 6 inches apart. Add pillows inside to keep the shoeboxes standing.

2 Begin by balancing a plank on each shoebox toward the other shoebox. You need to add a weight to the end of the plank that stays on the box. Using more planks and weights, keep building the ends of your bridge toward each other.

. DID YOU KNOW? . . . . .

The Howrah Bridge in West Bengal, India, is the busiest cantilever bridge in the world. Approximately 100,000 vehicles and more than 150,000 pedestrians use it daily.

3 Can you add a final plank to connect the two ends into a complete bridge? Where do you need to place the weights to keep the bridge balanced?

4 Test your bridge by adding different loads. Try varying the way the planks are stacked. What can you do to get them to hold more weight?

TRY THIS: What happens if you use different lengths of blocks or other objects to make a cantilever bridge? Keep track of your designs in your notebook and decide on the best one.

CHAPTER 4

LET THE BUILDING BEGIN!

How does an engineer know the best place to build a bridge? What materials do they need to build it? How long will it take to build? How many workers will be needed? And, perhaps most importantly, how much will it cost to build this bridge?

Materials, time, manpower, and cost are just some of the many factors that need to be figured out before bridge construction can start. And even before these things can be decided on, the civil engineer must come up with a plan for the bridge. They need to approach the plan using the engineering design process.

WORDS TO KNOW

manpower: the number of people required to do a service or complete a project.

You have learned a lot about the engineering design process and done several activities using this method. Let's take a look at some of the other things engineers and builders think about when constructing a bridge.

THE STRENGTH OF THE FOUNDATION

An important consideration when designing a bridge is the type of land the bridge supports will be resting on. Will it be soft sand? Hard bedrock? Is it shells and rocks that might seem solid but can shift? A bridge is only as secure as its foundation. Engineers need to make sure that they have the best plan for the type of land they encounter.

WORDS ᴛᴏ KNOW

bedrock: the layer of solid rock deep underground, under the top layer of soil and loose rock.

survey: an examination of a site to gather information before building on it.

project manager: the person in charge of a project.

project surveyor: the person who surveys a project.

INVESTIGATE!

What is the process for building a bridge?

Once the survey is complete, the project manager, civil engineer, and project surveyor review the information and decide on the best type of bridge to build. The next step is to figure out the materials they will use to build the bridge.

laser: a device that emits a focused beam of light.

theodolite: a digital reader that gives the horizontal and vertical measurements of a bridge site.

WORDS TO KNOW

MATERIALS MAKE THE BRIDGE

How do engineers decide what types of materials to use when building a bridge? You might think that engineers always choose the strongest or the least expensive materials. But other factors are also important, such as how materials react to hot or cold weather.

Many bridges have been built with wood. Wood is solid, easy to work with, and cheap. Bridges that need to support a great number of heavy vehicles day in and day out, however, need to be made of something stronger. Today, the main choices for high-traffic bridges are concrete or steel.

DID YOU KNOW?

More than 2 billion tons of concrete are produced every year.

SURVEY SAYS!

Before a bridge can be designed, a survey of the proposed building site is conducted. If the bridge will be placed over a river, then the engineer needs to know the angle of the riverbank. If it will go between mountains, the engineer needs to understand the depth of the valley below. Surveyors use different electronic measuring devices, such as an automatic level, which give them the accurate distance from one side to another. They also use laser measuring devices to get exact lengths and depths. Some surveyors use a tool called a theodolite that can measure both horizontal and vertical aspects of the bridge site.

CONCRETE SUPPORTS

gravel: crushed bits of rock.

brittle: easily broken, cracked, or snapped.

WORDS ⓽ KNOW

Concrete has been around for a long time. It is strong, solid, and can be used to make bridges that last for many years. Most importantly, it costs less than steel.

This material is relatively easy to make. It is made of cement, sand, and gravel. When cement, sand, gravel, and water are combined together in a certain way, the mixture hardens and makes concrete.

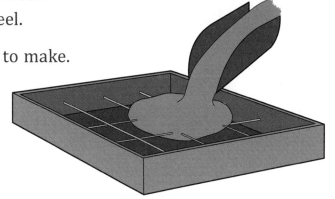

Concrete by itself can be brittle, which means that it breaks easily when under tension. That doesn't sound like good material for a bridge!

Construction workers add bars of steel to concrete to make it strong. These bars make the concrete able to withstand greater compression force. Concrete with steel bars inside is called pre-stressed concrete. Pre-stressed concrete has been used in bridges since 1950. It is the number-one choice for engineers when constructing a bridge.

Pre-stressed concrete is also able to be molded into practically any shape imaginable! And it is much less expensive than steel. Why would you not use pre-stressed concrete? Concrete needs a long time to harden to become strong. Steel, on the other hand, is strong from the beginning. Let's take a look at why an engineer might use steel in their bridge.

STEEL SUPPORTS

Steel is the second-most-used material for building bridges. It is able to hold lots of traffic day after day, and it lasts for many years.

Steel is a ductile material. That means that it can stretch when under pressure. Inspectors can see if a steel bridge is bending or buckling and take steps to fix it. But concrete is brittle, and can crack from excessive force without notice. In this way, steel bridges can be safer.

The best part about using steel for a bridge is that it's faster to build a steel bridge than a concrete bridge. Concrete takes time to harden, or cure. The minimum time needed for concrete to cure is 28 days. That means the concrete girders cannot be put into place for at least a month after they are made!

Steel is composed of iron ore that is dug from the ground and heated to an extremely high temperature. This process is called smelting. Smelting turns the iron ore into liquid iron.

After being mixed with other elements, such as carbon, to make steel, the mixture is then poured into a mold in the form of a girder. Once it has cooled and hardened, the girder is ready to be used to make a bridge or a building.

Why isn't steel used more often? Steel is very heavy compared to concrete. Steel can also rust. Rusting happens when steel is exposed to salt, moisture, and oxygen for long periods of time. As the chemicals in the steel break down, the steel weakens.

element: a pure substance that cannot be broken down into a simpler substance. Everything in the universe is made up of combinations of elements. Oxygen, gold, and carbon are three elements.

carbon: an element found in living things, including plants. Carbon is also found in diamonds, charcoal, and graphite.

rust: a coating that forms on iron or steel due to breakdown from oxidation.

zinc: a metallic element found in rocks.

WORDS TO KNOW

PAINTING AWAY RUST

Steel bridges sometimes look red or green, but that is not the true color of steel! These bridges are painted. Why paint a bridge? Just to make it look better? Sometimes, that is the reason, but they are also painted because the paint contains zinc, a mineral that helps keep the steel bridge from rusting. A dozen men have the job of painting the Golden Gate Bridge over and over again. They climb up to the top of its 746-foot towers and crawl in all of its tiny openings to get every spot. Considering that there are more than 600,000 bolts holding the bridge together, that's a pretty big job!

comptroller: a person responsible for the financial accounting of a project.

WORDS TO KNOW

MANPOWER, TIME, AND COST

Another part of the plan that engineers consider is the number of people needed to build the bridge. How many workers, trucks, cranes, and supplies will be needed? While it can be difficult to know exactly how many people help build bridges, the number can be in the thousands.

How long does it take to build a bridge? It took more than four years to build the Golden Gate Bridge in San Francisco. It took eight years to build the Tower Bridge in London. It all depends on the length of the bridge, the type of bridge, the materials, and how many people work on it.

Who will pay for the new bridge? Will it be the state? Will it be the federal government? Perhaps both will contribute a certain amount of money. On most bridge projects, a person called a comptroller pays attention to the money.

DID YOU KNOW?

The U.S. Navy wanted the Golden Gate Bridge to be painted with big gold and black stripes to make it more visible!

They are in charge of keeping track of how the money is spent and where all the money goes. This is a very important part of the plan.

Sometimes, bridges are not built because there is no money in the state or federal budget. Lack of money is also the reason old bridges fall into disrepair. Sometimes, old bridges are not replaced, but simply patched up and re-painted.

PERMISSION TO BUILD

The final step in the planning process is to get permits from the state or national government to construct the bridge. A permit gives permission to the project manager to begin building the bridge.

WHAT DO YOU GET WHEN YOU CROSS A RIVER?

Wet.

Once the engineer has a permit, it's time to build! It takes months and even years to complete a bridge. Some bridges are brand new and span areas that have never seen a bridge. Others are built to replace current bridges. A bridge might even be built right next to the old one. Whatever the type of bridge and its location, one thing is sure—it must be safe!

CONSIDER AND DISCUSS

It's time to consider and discuss: What is the process for building a bridge?

SOIL SAMPLES

The type of soil a bridge will stand on plays a huge part in how a bridge is supported. Get ready to dig in and get your hands dirty!

1 Glue the four wooden dowels to one side of the balsa wood, one at each corner. You have made a simple table-like structure. This is your bridge.

2 Place the bridge in the sandbox. Measure the depth of the sand with your ruler and record it in your notebook.

3 While your bridge is resting on the sand, place the empty bowl on it. What happens? Does the bridge sink? Does the bridge appear wobbly at all? Write down your observations.

4 Now, add water to the bowl. Take measurements again. Did the bridge sink further? Try to wobble the bridge. Can you? Push the bridge all the way to the floor of the sandbox or cardboard box. Now try to wobble it. Does it get harder? What does this show you about how deep the piers need to be when building a bridge?

TRY THIS: Use different materials for your soil: dirt, gravel, or powdered sugar. What is the best combination for supporting the bridge?

CABLE STRENGTH

A suspension or cable-stayed bridge is only as strong as the cables supporting it. Just how strong do the cables have to be?

SUPPLIES

* 2 stacks of books of even height
* 20 strands of uncooked spaghetti
* hole punch
* plastic cup
* string
* paper clip
* weights such as pennies or sugar cubes
* engineering notebook and pencil

1 Set up your book stacks so that they are close enough for a single strand of spaghetti to stretch between them and be held within the pages.

2 Poke two holes across from each other along the upper part of the plastic cup. Run the string through the holes to make a bucket.

3 Hang the paper clip off of the spaghetti strand. Attach the plastic cup to the paper clip with the string.

4 Add weights to the cup until the strand breaks. How many weights does it take? Record your observations in your notebook.

5 Repeat, using a group of five strands of spaghetti. Can it hold more weights?

THINK MORE: Why do you think the cables supporting the bridge are so thick? When the Incas built their rope bridges, why did they twist their materials together to make the ropes thicker?

REINFORCING CONCRETE

Concrete is strong, but we can make it stronger! Give it a try!

1 With your clay, make two bricks that are about ½ inch thick and 4 inches long.

2 Into one of the bricks, push two or three popsicle sticks horizontally. You might have to mold the clay around the popsicle sticks. Let your bricks dry overnight.

3 Set up your book supports in two even piles. Position the brick without the wooden sticks as a bridge across the books.

4 Start a scientific method worksheet in your notebook. Which brick will be able to support more weight? Record your hypothesis.

5 Poke two holes across from each other along the upper part of your plastic cup with the hole punch.

6 Thread a piece of string through the cup. Tie the other end of the string around the brick. The cup should be hanging below the brick a few inches off the ground.

7 Add a few tablespoons of sand to the plastic cup. What happens to your brick?

8 Continue adding sand, keeping track of how much you've added, until your brick breaks. Record how many tablespoons of weight the bridge was able to hold.

9 Repeat the process with the brick with the wooden sticks. Was the second brick able to hold more sand? Record your results. If so, why do you think that is?

THINK MORE: How would this experiment change if you added a live load? How might supports need to react differently to a load that moves?

COMPARING BRIDGE TYPES

You have now built many different types of bridges. Which one is the best one? Which holds more of a load? Which is more flexible? Which is easiest to construct?

1 Make a chart in your notebook with three columns. The first column on the left is the name of the bridge. The next column should have the number of weights that it can support. The final column will have the number of weights it takes to collapse the bridge.

2 Now, test each bridge with the weights. Keep adding weight until the bridge collapses.

3 Record your observations in your engineering notebook. Compare your results. What did you find?

THINK MORE: Did the bridges that are supposed to be the strongest actually support the most weight? If they didn't, why not?

FIXED VS. TEMPORARY

The strength of a bridge depends on its structure and its purpose. A bridge that is fixed is supposed to remain in place for many years and needs to be quite strong. Bridges that are temporary, for example, a bridge that is in place while another bridge is being repaired, need to last only a short while. Better hope your engineer knows the difference!

CHAPTER 5

FAMOUS BRIDGES

Bridges are found everywhere in the world, on almost every continent. Some bridges stretch for miles, while others are short and cross only small rivers or streams. Most bridges are made just for keeping transportation flowing. A few of them soar to amazing heights and are easily recognizable by a picture.

What makes a bridge famous? It might be the way the bridge looks. It may have an interesting engineering design. Or maybe the history of the bridge makes it recognizable to people all around the world. Let's take a look at some of the most famous bridges in the world.

? INVESTIGATE!

Why do some bridges become famous?

GOLDEN GATE BRIDGE, SAN FRANCISCO, CALIFORNIA

The Golden Gate Bridge is a suspension bridge that connects the city of San Francisco with the city of Sausalito. The bridge was built in 1937 and is 1.7 miles long.

(CREDIT: RICH NIEWIROSKI JR.)

The two massive towers that hold up the deck are 726 feet high and weigh more than 44,000 tons. The entire bridge is made of more than 88,000 tons of steel. The Golden Gate Bridge is the eleventh-longest bridge in the world.

One thing engineers had to consider when building the Golden Gate Bridge was wind. Have you ever been outside on a extremely windy day? Wind can be extremely strong. The force of a strong wind can knock over a tree during a storm.

DID YOU KNOW?

It costs $7.50 for a car or motorcycle to pass over the Golden Gate Bridge, but it costs a truck with three axles $22.50 for a one-way trip. Pedestrians and bicyclists may use the sidewalks for free.

If the wind comes from a tornado or hurricane, it might be strong enough to flip cars and trucks. It can even cause a bridge to twist or buckle or be torn apart.

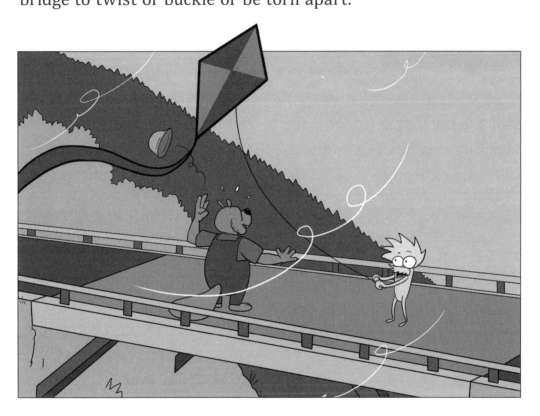

Extreme weather events are not the only reason wind is dangerous on a bridge. High winds can actually blow the cars and trucks around on the bridge as they drive across. That makes it dangerous to drive. Sounds pretty scary, doesn't it?

Don't worry! Every bridge has a maximum wind warning. When the winds reach that point, the bridge is closed to traffic. This might make some people angry at having to drive the long way around, but it keeps people safe.

Wind also causes suspension and cable-stayed bridges, such as the Golden Gate Bridge, to sway back and forth. On very rare occasions, a bridge can sway enough to reach a state called resonance. Resonance occurs when very tiny vibrations in the bridge all happen in sync, or at the same exact time. These tiny back-and-forth movements match up with the bridge materials' natural vibrations. When that happens, the bridge can actually shake itself apart! However, this is extremely rare.

TOWER BRIDGE, LONDON, UNITED KINGDOM

The Tower Bridge was built in 1894 and stretches 938 feet over the River Thames. It is a bascule bridge. A bascule is sort of like a see-saw that you might see in a park. The center portion is set on cantilever trusses. The deck is split into two parts, which can be angled upward for ships to pass through.

counter-weight: equal weights that cause an object to be balanced.

WORDS TO KNOW

As the decks tilt up, counter-weights on the lower ends keep the decks balanced. The Tower Bridge is one of the most visited places in the world.

SYDNEY HARBOUR BRIDGE, SYDNEY, AUSTRALIA

The Sydney Harbour Bridge is the third-most recognizable bridge in the world. This arched bridge is made entirely out of steel. The largest arch bridge in the world, it stands more than 439 feet over the water in Sydney Harbour. That's about half the height of the Empire State Building in New York City! Construction began on the bridge in 1924 and lasted eight years. It took more than 1,400 men and $4.2 million to complete. In 2017, the same bridge would cost more than $58 million to build. That's a lot of money!

BRIDGES!

WORDS TO KNOW

pilings: posts used to hold up the structure of a building or bridge.

. **DID YOU KNOW?** . . . . . .

People who live in Sydney call the bridge the "Coat Hanger" because they think it looks like a big hanger people would hang a coat on.

The Sydney Harbor Bridge is also the world's largest steel arch bridge. Steel bridges are very strong, and yet, like all bridges, they could possibly collapse. How does a steel bridge collapse?

The collapse of a bridge can be caused by wind, weather, the amount of traffic, the type of soil it is built upon, or the materials themselves. Any one of these things by itself isn't always enough to make a bridge collapse, but when you combine a couple of problems, you might be looking at trouble. This was the case for the San Francisco-Oakland Bay Bridge, another famous steel bridge.

RIALTO BRIDGE, VENICE, ITALY

The Rialto Bridge is one of the oldest bridges in the world, built in 1591. It is only 24 feet across, but it's built on more than 12,000 wooden pilings that are sunk in the river.

Two walkways on the outer sides of the bridge move people past the middle section that is full of shops. The Rialto Bridge is one of the most famous sites in all of Venice and is visited by millions of tourists every year.

EARTHQUAKES!

Earthquakes can cause damage to all types of structures, including bridges. An earthquake happens when the ground shifts. This movement is caused by two pieces of the earth's crust, called tectonic plates, rubbing against each other.

The place where the two plates meet is called a fault line. Fault lines crisscross all over the world. When the land around a fault line moves, any structure nearby will feel this move, including bridges. Earthquakes have to be pretty strong to make a bridge come crashing down, but even smaller earthquakes can cause damage.

crust: the outer, thin layer of the earth.

tectonic plate: a large section of the earth's crust that moves on top of the hot, melted layer below.

fault line: the intersection of two tectonic plates.

Richter scale: the scale used to measure the strength of an earthquake.

WORDS TO KNOW

Sometimes, the piers develop cracks or the soil under the piers becomes unstable. Perhaps the bolts that hold the bridge together are loosened. Bridges that are located near where earthquakes have taken place are carefully inspected for any type of wear or damage.

In 1989, the area of Loma Prieta in California experienced a 6.9-magnitude earthquake out of 10.0 on the Richter scale. While the earthquake lasted only 15 seconds, it did some major damage, including causing the top section of the San Francisco-Oakland Bay Bridge to collapse onto the lower deck. Since then, billions of dollars have been spent in the area to make sure all the bridges are in good repair. Part of the San Francisco-Oakland Bay Bridge was rebuilt between 2002 and 2013.

  PS You can watch a time-lapse video of the bridge project at this website.

KEYWORD PROMPTS

San Francisco-Oakland Bay Bridge time lapse 🔍

CHENGYANG WIND AND RAIN BRIDGE, CHENGYANG, CHINA

This wooden bridge is somewhat unique in that it was built with no nails or rivets. Each part connects to another, similar to puzzle pieces. There are five pillars and three beams that make up the bridge. The bridge itself has three stories. People can walk, talk, or relax on the open pavilions on each story. The roofs of the bridge are called pagodas and are completely covered in tiles.

The Chengyang Wind and Rain Bridge has been in use since 1912 and is in outstanding condition. It is shorter than most of the other famous bridges at only 211 feet.

(CREDIT: GILL_PENNEY)

SHELTER IN A STORM

When you think of staying safe in a storm, do you ever think of running to a bridge to do so? If you are near Chengyang, you might! The Chengyang Wind and Rain Bridge is so named because it provides shelter for the local people during a storm. It is also a place for them to gather and socialize. The bridge is not used just for access from one village to another, it is also a destination by itself.

Bridges are amazing structures. They allow us to travel to places that cannot be reached by foot, crossing over rivers, lakes, streams, estuaries, gorges, and other roads. They also connect islands, peninsulas, and cays. Bridges give us access to remote places in jungles, deserts, and beaches. They are part of our everyday life.

How many bridges do you cross over a day? A week? A year? Count them. You might be surprised to find out how important bridges are in your life!

CONSIDER AND DISCUSS

It's time to consider and discuss: Why do some bridges become famous?

WORDS TO KNOW

peninsula: a piece of land that juts out into water.

cay: a low-lying island formed by a reef.

WINDY DAY

Do you love the feel of wind blowing through your hair? While it may be fun for you, wind is not always the best thing for bridges. Let's see how blowing breezes affect a bridge.

SUPPLIES

* wooden sticks
* glue
* connecting building blocks
* electric fan
* tape measure
* engineering notebook and pencil

1 Build a bridge out of wooden sticks and glue. It can be a simple beam bridge, an arch bridge, or whatever type of bridge you want. You can even use one of the bridges that you have already made.

2 Build another bridge just like the first, with the connecting building blocks.

DID YOU KNOW?

Bridges are closed if the winds in the area reach just 40 miles per hour.

3 Set the bridges on a table or on the floor about 6 feet away from the fan. Which bridge will last longer in strong wind? Start a scientific method worksheet and record your hypothesis in your notebook.

4 Turn the fan on. Do the bridges move at all? If so, how much? Record your observations of each bridge in your engineering notebook.

5 Now, move the fan closer to the bridges. Try 3 feet, then 1 foot, then 6 inches. Make sure the speed of the fan is the same. What do you notice?

TRY THIS: Change the setting of your fan. Does this affect your bridges?

PROJECT!

SHAKING AND SHIVERING

A lot of shaking and vibrating can happen during earthquakes! This experiment helps you understand what type of vibrations a structure experiences during an earthquake.

1 Make the Jell-O in the mold according to the directions on the package.

2 Put the plate on top of the hardened Jell-O in the mold and flip the whole thing over. Gently remove the mold. You should have a free-standing Jell-O shape!

WHOSE FAULT IS IT THAT THE OAKLAND BAY BRIDGE IN CALIFORNIA COLLAPSED?

HA HA HA

San Andreas fault and Salton Trough fault, of course!

3 Place the giant marshmallow on top of the Jell-O. Shake the Jell-O. What happens to the marshmallow?

4 Now, secure the marshmallow to the Jell-O by putting two toothpicks through it, down into the Jell-O.

5 Shake the Jell-O again. What happens? Try to replace the marshmallow with different materials. What happens?

THINK MORE: What does this tell you about the best materials to use for bridges in places that have lots of earthquakes?

TEST IT OUT

Sometimes, engineers need to test different types of materials and their stress points. They need to know how much load a material can handle. Use the engineering design process to learn how making changes to materials can make them stronger or more brittle.

1 Make two bridges by placing a piece of paper across two stacks of two books each and a piece of construction paper set across the same combination of book stacks. Which bridge do you think can hold the most weight? Why?

2 Add the weights to the middle of each bridge. If you add one coin to the paper bridge, add one coin to the construction paper bridge and so on, until both bridges collapse. Make a note in your notebook of the number of weights it took to make each bridge fail.

3 Now brainstorm different materials to use for the deck. What about a piece of plastic? Or maybe a piece of wood? Evaluate how each of these materials may affect the strength of the bridge.

4 Test your prototypes and take notes on each one. If one fails, brainstorm a new material and give that a try. Think like an engineer and don't give up!

THINK MORE: How can you add more support to your bridge to it can hold more weight?

BUILD THE RIALTO BRIDGE

The Rialto Bridge is famous for being so old. Would this same type of bridge be built today? Would businesses be allowed to open on the bridge? You can make a model of the Rialto in this activity.

SUPPLIES
* clay that hardens when dry
* wooden craft sticks
* glue
* weights, such as coins or marbles

1 Mold the clay into a small arched bridge.

2 Before your bridge dries, use the craft sticks to create the shops in the center of this inhabited bridge. Be creative. Do you make one long shop or many individual ones?

DID YOU KNOW?

Venice, Italy, is made up of more than 118 islands and is connected by 400 footbridges and 170 boat canals.

3 Don't forget to leave an area for the walkways on either side. Construct railings for both sides of the bridge. You don't want your pedestrians falling off!

4 Let your bridge dry overnight. Then, add some weight to it in the form of coins or marbles. Is the stone bridge strong or does it fall down? If it does, start over.

TRY THIS: Add load at different places on the bridge. Is one position stronger than another?

SUPPLIES

* connecting building blocks

CHENGYANG WIND AND RAIN BRIDGE

For this project, you are going to try to copy the design of the Chengyang Bridge. The challenge is to do it the way the engineers did in 1912.

1 Take a look at the picture of the Chengyang Wind and Rain Bridge on page 72. Notice how the deck is balanced on the piers.

2 Build five piers with your blocks. Use longer blocks to attach three beams to just the five piers. Is it difficult to balance them?

3 Add in the superstructure of the Chengyang Wind and Rain Bridge. Can you make the railings with the benches for seats? How long does it take you to build this? How long do you think it took the engineers to build the bridge?

THINK MORE: Imagine that you are back in 1912. What types of materials and tools would you have to help you?

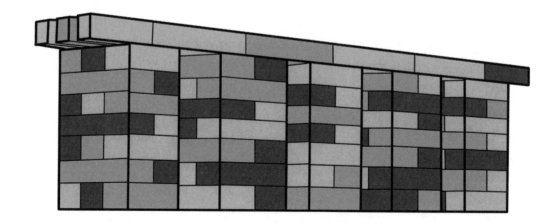

welding: joining together metal pieces or parts by heating the surfaces to the point of melting and pressing them together.

WORDS ⊚ KNOW

MATERIALS AND CONSTRUCTION

The Chengyang Bridge is made up of three different types of materials, but they all fit together perfectly like a great big puzzle. The piers are made of stone, the upper structures and handrails are made of wood, and the roof is covered in tiles.

Selecting the right materials is extremely important to bridge design and safety. It is not easy to build a bridge, and it can be quite dangerous—sometimes, a bridge collapses while it's being built. Some styles of bridge, such as the cantilever, need to be balanced just right. All of the weight must be supported by one pier. What if that pier is not fully secured at the bottom? That could mean disaster for the whole bridge.

Sometimes, the material that is used for the bridge has flaws. For example, in 1967, a bridge in Ohio collapsed because of a problem in one of the steel beams. At the factory where the steel beam was created, the beam was accidently made too weak for the bridge.

Human error is another reason bridges collapse. Failure to follow the exact design plans or using the wrong welding techniques can make beams weak and cause them to buckle. However, this doesn't happen very often!

BUILD THE GOLDEN GATE BRIDGE

You will build your own Golden Gate Bridge. Take a look at the picture of the bridge on page 66. Can you construct your own model of the bridge? How can you make sure it will stay standing in wind?

1 The first part you need to build is the deck. Construct the deck with the craft sticks. You can place them horizontally or diagonally.

2 Cut the balsa wood to fit and glue it to the top of your deck.

3 Stand up your shoe boxes for the support piers. You can cut a slit about halfway down into the boxes and slide your deck into them slightly. This will give the deck a small amount of support.

4 On the top of one box, tape one end of your string.

5 Stretch the string in a diagonal arc down to the deck. Attach it in the middle with tape. Don't cut it.

6 Now, continue the string to the top of the other box. Attach the string there with tape. Cut the string.

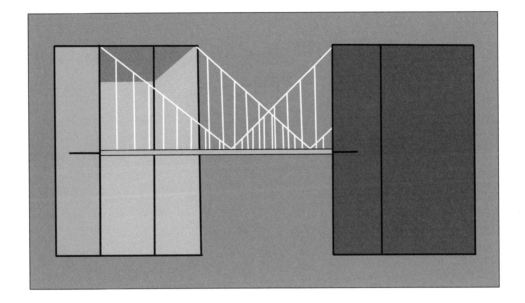

7 Repeat the same process on the other side. This is your supporting cable.

8 Take pieces of string and periodically attach them from the supporting cable straight down to the deck. These are the small supporting cables.

9 Continue to do this until your bridge is built. It should end up looking like the Golden Gate Bridge.

EXPLORE MORE: Brainstorm how you can make the Golden Gate Bridge stronger. What would you do to make it more stable during an earthquake? How could you make it safer during high winds? Give your ideas a try!

GLOSSARY GAME

Pick up a pencil and get a friend or two to explore the ideas in this book by filling out this silly Mad Lib game.

- **noun:** a person, place, or thing

- **adjective:** a word that describes a noun

- **verb:** an action word

- **adverb:** a word that describes a verb

I come upon a river. How will I _____ ? Should I _____ ? Should I _____ ?
VERB VERB VERB

I know! I'll _____ a bridge. I will need _____ and _____ .
VERB NOUN NOUN

What type of bridge will I _____ ?
VERB

It can be an _____ bridge or a _____ bridge.
NOUN NOUN

But it must be _____ enough to hold a _____ and a _____ . This will
ADJECTIVE NOUN NOUN

be a very _____ bridge. Where is the best place to _____ it? How stable is
ADJECTIVE VERB

the _____ ? How _____ will it have to be? How long _____ it take?
NOUN ADJECTIVE VERB

Whatever I _____ , it needs to be a _____ one.
VERB ADJECTIVE

I have to get home!

abutment: a structure on which a bridge rests, such as a pier.

anchorage: a strong vertical support for a suspension bridge.

angle: the space between two lines that start from the same point, measured in degrees.

arch: a curved structure in the shape of an upside-down U or semi-circle.

arch bridge: a bridge formed with a curved support as its main component.

bascule bridge: a bridge with a section that pivots like a see-saw.

BCE: put after a date, BCE stands for Before Common Era and counts down to zero. CE stands for Common Era and counts up from zero. These nonreligious terms correspond to BC and AD. This book was printed in 2018 CE.

beam: a rigid piece of the structure that carries the load.

beam bridge: a bridge with a horizontal beam across two vertical supports.

bedrock: the layer of solid rock deep underground, under the top layer of soil and loose rock.

bridge: a structure built to cross something that blocks your way, such as a river, bay, road, railway, or valley.

brittle: easily broken, cracked, or snapped.

buckle: to collapse in the middle.

cable-stayed bridge: a bridge that uses a cable connected from the deck to one or more vertical columns.

cantilever: a beam with one end supported and the other end free.

cantilever bridge: a bridge that uses diagonal cantilever supports, and sometimes trusses.

canyon: a deep trench in the earth, often with steep sides.

carbon: an element found in living things, including plants. Carbon is also found in diamonds, charcoal, and graphite.

cast: to create a shape by pouring liquid into a mold and allowing it to harden.

cay: a low-lying island formed by a reef.

characteristic: a feature of a person, place, or thing.

civilization: a community of people that is advanced in art, science, and government.

collapse: to fall in or down suddenly.

compression: a pushing force that squeezes or presses a material inward.

comptroller: a person responsible for the financial accounting of a project.

concrete: a hard construction material made with cement, sand, and water.

counter-weight: equal weights that cause an object to be balanced.

crust: the outer, thin layer of the earth.

cure: to harden an object such as cement or concrete.

data: information gathered during an experiment.

dead load: the weight of a structure itself.

debris: the remains of anything broken down or destroyed.

deck: the horizontal part of a bridge, where the cars go over.

diagonal: a straight line joining two opposite corners of a square, rectangle, or other straight-sided shape.

ductile: describes a material that can change, stretch, and bend while not breaking.

durable: lasting a long time.

element: a pure substance that cannot be broken down into a simpler substance. Everything in the universe is made up of combinations of elements. Oxygen, gold, and carbon are three elements.

engineer: a person who uses science, math, and creativity to design and build things.

engineering: the use of science and math in the design and construction of things.

erode: to wear away rock or soil by water and wind.

estuary: a partly enclosed coastal body of water, which has rivers and streams flowing into it and is connected to the ocean.

fault line: the intersection of two tectonic plates.

feat: an achievement that requires great courage, skill, or strength.

flood stage: the point where water in a river or stream overflows its banks.

footings: the foundations of a structure, such as a bridge or building.

force: a push or pull applied to an object.

foundation: the supporting part of a structure, found usually at the bottom.

girder: a support beam.

goods: items, such as food and clothing, that people can buy and sell.

gravel: crushed bits of rock.

gravity: the force that pulls all objects to the earth's surface.

horizontal: straight across from side to side.

Inca: South American people who lived from the thirteenth to the sixteenth century. They built Machu Picchu, a famous fortress.

inflexible: rigid and unyielding.

infrastructure: roads, bridges, and other basic types of structures and equipment needed for a country to function properly.

inhabit: to live in a certain place.

interconnected: when two or more things are related or have an impact on each other.

interval: a standard space between objects.

iron: a strong, hard, magnetic metal.

iron ore: rocks and minerals that contain iron.

laser: a device that emits a focused beam of light.

live load: the weight of the objects moving across a structure.

load: an object that puts weight on another object.

logo: a symbol used to identify a company, which appears on its products and in its marketing.

maintenance: to keep something working and in good shape.

manpower: the number of people required to do a service or complete a project.

maximum: the highest or greatest amount possible.

mortar: a building material that hardens when it dries, like glue. It is used to hold bricks and stones together.

natural bridge: a bridge created by the natural formation of rock or land.

obstacle: something that blocks you from what you want to achieve.

pagoda: a structure that looks like a tower that is decorated and has curving roofs.

pavilion: a park or garden that is open on the sides.

pedestrian: a person walking to get from one place to another.

peninsula: a piece of land that juts out into water.

permit: a written order allowing for an action to be done.

pier: a supporting pillar or post.

pilings: posts used to hold up the structure of a building or bridge.

project manager: the person in charge of a project.

project surveyor: the person who surveys a project.

prototype: a model of something that allows engineers to test their ideas.

railway bridge: a bridge that is built to carry trains.

reinforced concrete: concrete that contains iron bars to make it stronger.

resonance: when tiny vibrations happen inside materials or structures at the same time.

Richter scale: the scale used to measure the strength of an earthquake.

rust: a coating that forms on iron or steel due to breakdown from oxidation.

shear: a sliding force that slips parts of a material in opposite directions.

smelt: to remove iron from iron ore through heat and melting.

soil composition: the bits of minerals, rocks, and dirt that are present in the soil.

span: to stretch from side to side of something. Also, the distance between two things.

stable: steady and firm, not changing.

steel: a hard, strong material made of iron combined with other elements.

substructure: the support areas beneath a bridge.

superstructure: the support areas above a bridge.

survey: an examination of a site to gather information before building on it.

suspended central truss: a truss section added to the middle of a bridge for extra support.

GLOSSARY

suspension bridge: a bridge that uses ropes or cables from a vertical support to hold the weight of the deck and traffic.

technology: the tools, methods, and systems used to solve a problem or do work.

tectonic plate: a large section of the earth's crust that moves on top of the hot, melted layer below.

tension: a pulling force that pulls or stretches a material outward.

theodolite: a digital reader that gives the horizontal and vertical measurements of a bridge site.

torrential: violent, heavy rain.

torsion: a twisting force that turns or twirls a material.

trade: to exchange goods for other goods or money.

truss bridge: a bridge design that uses diagonal posts above or below the bridge to provide extra support.

trusses: diagonal beams added to a bridge for extra support.

vertical: straight up and down.

volcanic: from lava that came out of a volcano.

waste: unwanted material that can harm the environment.

welding: joining together metal pieces or parts by heating the surfaces to the point of melting and pressing them together.

wind tunnel: a huge circular tunnel where scientists use manmade wind to test its effect on objects.

zinc: a metallic element found in rocks.

METRIC CONVERSIONS

Use this chart to find the metric equivalents to the English measurements in this book. If you need to know a half measurement, divide by two. If you need to know twice the measurement, multiply by two. How do you find a quarter measurement? How do you find three times the measurement?

English	Metric
1 inch	2.5 centimeters
1 foot	30.5 centimeters
1 yard	0.9 meter
1 mile	1.6 kilometers
1 pound	0.5 kilogram
1 teaspoon	5 milliliters
1 tablespoon	15 milliliters
1 cup	237 milliliters

86

BOOKS

Enz, Tammy. *Building Bridges (Young Engineers)*. Heinemann. 2017.

Keely, Cheryl. *A Book of Bridges: Here to There and Me to You*. Sleeping Bear Press. 2017.

Hoena, Blake. *Building the Golden Gate Bridge: An Interactive Engineering Adventure (You Choose: Engineering Marvels)*. Capstone Press. 2014.

Latham, Donna. *Bridges and Tunnels: Investigate Feats of Engineering with 25 Projects (Build It Yourself)*. Nomad Press. 2012.

Loh-Hagan Edd, Virginia. *Bridges (21st Century Junior Library: Extraordinary Engineering)*. Cherry Lake Publishing. 2017.

Marsico, Katie. *Bridges (True Bookengineering Wonders)*. C. Press/F. Watts Trade. 2016.

Stine, Megan. *Where Is the Brooklyn Bridge?* Grosset & Dunlap. 2016.

WEBSITES

Building Big by PBS Kids: Learn the basics of bridge building and even try to complete a building challenge.
pbs.org/wgbh/buildingbig/bridge

Engineering Games by PBS Kids: Learn to think like an engineer and put your skills to the test!
pbskids.org/games/engineering

Try Engineering: Games and activities to stimulate the engineering brain in all of us.
tryengineering.org/play-games

Build a Bridge with NOVA: Learn the steps to bridge building and then give it a try yourself.
pbs.org/wgbh/nova/tech/build-bridge-p1.html

QR CODE GLOSSARY

Page 13: youtube.com/watch?v=pvo4iLDAERg

Page 25: commons.wikimedia.org/w/index.
php?title=File%3ATacoma_Narrows_Bridge_destruction.ogv

Page 39: amusingplanet.com/2012/06/10-largest-natural-arches-in-world.html

Page 71: youtube.com/watch?v=GDUIYZKlknk

ESSENTIAL QUESTIONS

Introduction: Why do we need different types of bridges for different purposes?

Chapter 1: Why are bridges important? What might
the world be like without bridges?

Chapter 2: What do engineers need to think about when they design a bridge?

Chapter 3: How do engineers decide what type of bridge to build?

Chapter 4: What is the process for building a bridge?

Chapter 5: Why do some bridges become famous?

INDEX